The Golden Egg Book

By MARGARET WISE BROWN

Illustrated by LEONARD WEISGARD

A GOLDEN BOOK • NEW YORK

Copyright © 1947, renewed 1975 by Random House, Inc. All rights reserved under International and Pan-American Copyright Conventions. Published in the United States by Golden Books, an imprint of Random House Children's Books, a division of Random House, Inc., New York, and simultaneously in Canada by Random House of Canada Limited, Toronto. Originally published in 1947 in different form by Simon & Schuster, Inc., and Artists and Writers Guild, Inc. Golden Books, A Golden Book, Big Little Golden Book, the G colophon, and the distinctive gold spine are registered trademarks of Random House, Inc. Library of Congress Control Number: 2003104103
ISBN: 0-375-82717-X (trade)—ISBN: 0-375-92503-1 (lib. bdg.)
www.goldenbooks.com
Printed in the United States of America   First Random House Edition 2004
10 9 8 7 6

Visit us on the Web! www.randomhouse.com/kids
Educators and librarians, for a variety of teaching tools, visit us at
www.randomhouse.com/teachers

Once there was a little bunny.
He was all alone.
One day he found an egg.
He could hear something moving
    inside the egg.
What was it?

Maybe a little boy,

Maybe another bunny,

Maybe an elephant,

Maybe a mouse.

Who could tell what he would find?
And how would a little bunny know?
But there was something
inside that egg.

He could hear
something moving.

He shook it.

Then the bunny
pushed the egg
with his foot.

He jumped on top
of the egg.

He climbed a tree and threw nuts at it.

He rolled the egg down a hill.
But still it didn't break.
And whatever was
in the egg
didn't come out.

So the bunny
    threw a rock
    at the egg.
But because he was only a
    little bunny, it was a very
    little rock and he didn't
    throw it very hard and
    the egg didn't break.

Pick

Pick

Pick

Something was trying to get out of that egg.
The bunny sat very still and watched
through his shining eyes.

He sat very still and listened
with his big soft ears—

Pick

Pick

Pick

Then the little bunny
began to yawn.
And he yawned
and he yawned.

The egg was
very quiet.

He curled up all sleepy and warm
close to the egg and went to sleep.
He went to sleep because he was
so sleepy.

Then . . .

Pick
    Pick
        Pick
and
    Peck
        Peck
        Peck

And crackety CRACK!
Out jumped a little yellow duck.

"Well, what is this?" said the little duck
when he saw the bunny.
"What could this little fur thing be?"

The bunny was very sleepy,
so he was still asleep
and didn't wake up.

"Inside the egg,"
said the duck,
"I thought I was all alone
in a small dark world.

"Now I find myself alone with a bunny
in a big bright world.
And the bunny won't wake up."

So the duck pushed th

unny with his foot

And jumped
on top of him

And threw a little rock
at him

And rolled him down a hill.

And the bunny woke up.
"Where is my egg?"
said the bunny.
"And where did you
come from?"

"Never mind that," said the duck.
"Here I am."
So the bunny and the duck
were friends

And no one was ever
alone again.